DEATH AT DUSK

Demon Hunter

Death at Dusk

Jason M. Burns

Darby Creek
Minneapolis

Darby Creek
An imprint of Lerner Publishing Group, Inc.
241 First Avenue North
Minneapolis, MN 55401 USA

For reading levels and more information, look up this title at www.lernerbooks.com.

Image credits: Ihor Hvozdetskyi/Shutterstock (mosquito); Kwangmoozaa/Shutterstock (mosquitoes); Rosen Graphic/Shutterstock (texture);idwan kurnia/Shutterstock (font); PERFECT_VECTORS/Shutterstock (font).

Main body text set in Janson Text LT Std.
Typeface provided by Adobe Systems.

Library of Congress Cataloging-in-Publication Data

Names: Burns, Jason M., 1978–author
Title: Death at dusk / Jason M. Burns.
Description: Minneapolis : Darby Creek, [2026] | Series: Demon hunter | Audience term: Teenagers | Audience: Ages 11–18 | Audience: Grades 7–9 | Summary: When bodies begin turning up drained of blood and missing their brains, demon-hunter Damon and his friends suspect a mosquito-formed demon and race to track it down before it strikes again.
Identifiers: LCCN 2025013049 (print) | LCCN 2025013050 (ebook) | ISBN 9798765670651 library binding | ISBN 9798348028183 paperback | ISBN 9798765691885 epub
Subjects: CYAC: Demons—Fiction | Mosquitoes—Fiction | Supernatural—Fiction | Friendship—Fiction | LCGFT: Paranormal fiction | Novels
Classification: LCC PZ7.1.B88535 Dc 2026 (print) | LCC PZ7.1.B88535 (ebook) | DDC [Fic]—dc23/eng/20250416

LC record available at https://lccn.loc.gov/2025013049
LC ebook record available at https://lccn.loc.gov/2025013050

Manufactured in the United States of America
1 – TR – 12/15/25

To Hunter and Eloise—hunt down what makes you happy in life and don't be afraid to face your demons.

1

I don't know why this time of year is called the dog days of summer. I think most people would agree that dogs are adorable balls of snuggle fur. How that same symbol of unconditional love and loyalty has anything to do with the hottest, most unbearable time of the year, I'll never understand.

I also don't know why the Salem charter of the Chickadee Scouts thinks this is the best time to schedule our annual camping trip. There is nothing fun about trying to sleep in a steamy tent with a group of teenage boys, half of whom have yet to master the art of applying deodorant.

With nearly 100 percent humidity and nighttime temperatures lingering around the 85-degree mark, I'm currently stewing in my own juices as my fellow Chickadees and I sit around the campfire telling ghost stories. My brown skin is streaked in sweat from head to toe. What I wouldn't give to have ten minutes in the freezer section at the local grocery store right about now.

"I'm serious," Kenny Haberlin claims as his spooky story draws to a close. If a ventriloquist lost their puppet just before going onstage, Kenny could sub in. His limbs hang off of him as if they were stapled on. "I heard it from my sister's friend who heard it from her cousin who heard it from his barber. It totally happened."

Neal Kemp, as long and as lean as a telephone pole, hurls a marshmallow at Kenny, bonking him on his head with the sugar-puffed treat. Neal has that looks-like-a-forty-year-old-at-sixteen sort of way. We have substitute teachers who look younger than him. "Get real! There's no such thing as werewolves! And I don't care whose barber says otherwise!"

I've been a Chickadee Scout since I was five years old. A lot of kids have come and gone over the years, but there's a core group of us—Neal and Kenny included—who have basically grown up together in the organization. None of us are super close nor do we really hang out outside of the Chickadees, but when we're on scouting trips, we all have a good time together. As we've gotten older, though, it seems like all we do is just egg each other on in some pointless attempt to one-up each other. It's kind of exhausting.

"Oh yeah?" Kenny says, tossing the marshmallow back at Neal. It hits Neal in the shoulder and rolls down his arm, landing at my feet. "If you're such a storyteller, why don't *you* tell the group something really scary?"

I pick the marshmallow up and toss it into the fire. My gaze rests on it as it bubbles and blackens in the flames. I'm perfectly fine just being a spectator rather than a participant. In fact, I never join in on this part of the annual camping trip.

The truth is that I have stories that would keep my fellow Chickadees awake for the rest of their lives. And mine are as real as that flaming marshmallow. I know because I've lived them. Some, I barely even survived.

It all began when I was a Hatchling Scout. (That's the younger version of the Chickadees.) I was just a kid when I realized I could see auras. An aura is like a personal fingerprint for the soul. Everyone's looks different. It was my mom who first discovered my gift and urged me to embrace it. She taught me to not just see auras, but to read them as well.

Reading an aura is like reading a person's biography. I can learn a ton about someone just by dissecting their aura with my eyes. For example, I can tell that Neal is sensitive, defensive about his sensitivity—and totally unrelated to either of the first two, also has sensitive teeth. (He really should use a special toothpaste to help with that last one.)

Neal sits up straight and puffs out his chest. The air is already thick enough because of the humidity level, but it's getting even more difficult to breathe around the roaring fire.

"My story would earn a spooky tale merit badge if there was one, Kenny," Neal says, just daring his fellow Chickadee to escalate the war of words. "And unlike yours, mine is actually true."

Kenny scoffs. "Let's hear it then, tough guy."

So yeah, I can read auras, but that's not the main reason why I don't participate in the scary story feud every year. It's just a small part of a larger—and much more complicated—equation.

See, I use my aura-reading ability to hunt demons. The majority of the world doesn't know that demons exist, but I don't have that luxury. I can't help but see demons as their auras look completely different from us humans. While ours are colorful and full of kaleidoscope designs, theirs are more like a stack of disorganized papers if each and every sheet of paper were as black as a shadow.

So *that's* the main reason why I don't tell any creepy tales on these trips. Part of the reason they all get to sleep so soundly every night is because my best friends, Liam and Madelyn, and I keep Salem safe from the real dangers.

I get up and stretch my legs. The pooled-up perspiration at the back of my knees runs down my calves.

"I'll be back," I say, turning away from the fire. "I'm going to go grab something from my tent. Keep telling your stories though. I'll be listening."

"Fine," Neal says, grinning from ear to ear. "I feel bad for whoever is sleeping next to Kenny tonight because he's definitely wetting his sleeping bag later."

I walk back to the tent to retrieve the homemade bug spray from my pack. It's basically a mixture of essential oils, including citronella and peppermint. My friend Madelyn has extremely sensitive skin, and it was a recipe her mother found on the internet. I started using it too because it smelled a lot better than the can of chemicals you can buy from the store, and it seems to work just as well.

As I reach my tent, I hear Neal start up his story.

"First off," he says, "I know this is true because it happened when my grandfather was our age. He lived through it, and he told me all about it. His barber had nothing to do with any of it."

I admire Neal's dig at Kenny as I unzip my tent and climb inside. I instantly notice a lump underneath my sprawled out sleeping bag.

"Anyway, it was 1950-something," Neal continues. "Salem was still Salem, but it was different in a lot of ways. There was still a lot of undeveloped land, and the swampy area out by the highway was a lot bigger. That meant there were a lot more mosquitoes buzzing around town."

I reach down and poke the lump with my finger. It squishes like a rotten piece of fruit. It has to be one of my fellow Chickadees trying to pull a prank on me. Like I said, we're always trying to one-up each other.

"But here's the thing," Neal goes on. "No one really worried about mosquitoes when my grandfather was a kid. Parents didn't douse their kids in insect repellent. No one ran and hid inside at dawn and dusk. At least at that time, mosquitoes were just . . . annoying. That all changed the summer my grandfather was set to enter his junior year of high school."

I turn around and zip the tent closed. If someone put something disgusting in my sleeping bag, I'm going to return the favor and hide it in a fellow Chickadee's stuff. Maybe in their pillowcase? That would certainly "one-up" them.

"First, some farmer out along the edge of town found one of his cows lying down in the pasture," Neal narrates as I grab hold of my sleeping bag, getting ready to pull back on it for the reveal. It had better not be a ball of shaving cream!

"The cow was completely mummified. And the thing is, cops didn't exactly have a forensics department back then, and while everyone was a little spooked, they officially called the dead cow an 'unspecified animal attack.' Because as you all know, there are plenty of animals around here that can suck every drop of blood out of a full-grown cow."

I pull back the sleeping bag. The reveal is far more upsetting than a ball of shaving cream. There's a stowaway in my tent—a nightmare demon!

No bigger than a squirrel, the beady-eyed beast lunges at me, latching onto my face.

I try to quietly peel it free as Neal continues

to entertain my fellow Chickadees around the fire.

"Anyway, a couple of days go by, and no more cows show up mummified. But then, some guy—a businessperson from out of town—is found alongside the road looking like a prune."

I fall down on my back while trying to extract the clinging demon, and Kenny's retainer case digs into my spine. I have to stifle my scream to avoid calling any attention to the tent.

"He had been changing a flat tire on his car when, apparently, the same 'unspecified animal' attacked him, too."

Nightmare demons are nasty buggers. It makes sense for this one to be lurking around a campground. They look for any opportunity to slip into someone while they're sleeping and cause nightmares. For them, that unconscious fear is food. They feed on it like s'mores.

"Not only was he drained of all his blood," Neal continues, "but his brain was gone—sucked right out of his skull like someone was using his head like a juice box."

"Gross!" I hear another camper blurt out as I manage to wrestle the nightmare demon off of my face.

If he thinks that's gross, he should try staring into the eyes of this little monster. It's like looking at a Chihuahua that has been wrapped in saltwater taffy and then rolled in dirt. It doesn't smell any better, either, but it's still an improvement from all the teenage boy scents locked in the tent.

I hold the nightmare demon out at arm's length as I dig through my pack with my free hand. The demon tries to claw at me to set itself free.

Neal goes on, not realizing there's a real scary story playing out only a few yards away. "The attacks continued for the rest of the summer and into the fall. Three more people and a bunch of additional farm animals turned up dead and bloodless. Gossip spread quickly. People around town started to suspect that a serial killer was responsible, but my grandfather knew otherwise."

I grab hold of a bottle and pull it out of my pack. It's my homemade bug spray. That won't work against this pest.

"He was out fishing in one of the swamps one morning and saw the killer with his own eyes," Neal says, his voice rising for effect. "It was just before dawn, and it appeared in front of him—not an 'unspecified animal' but a terrifying monster. It was sort of half-man, half-mosquito and easily seven feet tall."

I toss the bug spray down and dig farther into my pack. The nightmare demon begins to squeal.

"Damon, are you okay in there?" Kenny calls out.

I stuff my thumb into the nightmare demon's mouth to keep it from making any additional noise. Completely toothless, the demon gnaws on my thumb with its gums.

"Yup!" I shout back. "Just accidentally kneeled on your retainer case. Be out in a second."

Satisfied with my excuse, Neal continues with his tale. "So yeah, the mosquito man was surrounded by a cloud of smaller mosquitoes that went wherever it did. My grandfather looked right at it, and it looked right back at him before—POOF—disappearing into the swamp."

With my free hand, I locate the second bottle hidden away at the bottom of my pack. I pull it out, grateful that I brought a "just in case" batch of holy water with me. Anything blessed is like a superweapon against a demon.

"The next night was the first official frost of the season, and the attacks stopped," Neal says. He pauses, building the tension. It's expert-level storytelling and it works. The gathered Chickadees are silent. "Just like that."

I bite down on the cap with my teeth and open the bottle. The nightmare demon wriggles in my hand, continuing to slobber all over my thumb as it does.

"You picked the wrong camping trip to bring your bad dreams to," I whisper into what I assume is its earhole.

I splash the holy water onto the nightmare demon. Its button-like eyes, black as the night sky above, go wide. The creature begins to convulse.

"Nope!" I hear Kenny say. "There's no way that story is anything more than that . . . a story."

I cover the nightmare demon's mouth with my hand, silencing it as it bubbles and blackens like the marshmallow I tossed into the campfire.

Neal's offended voice responds back to Kenny. "If you don't believe me, you can look it up. There are all sorts of theories online about it. The case remains unsolved to this day, and no suspect was ever named."

The nightmare demon exhales, its warm breath passing through my fingers, and then silently implodes. What remains is a clump of white mush in my hand. It looks a lot like a ball of shaving cream.

"My grandfather would talk about it from time to time," Neal says as I unzip the tent and climb out. I won't tell you where I wiped what was left of the nightmare demon. Someone is in for a real surprise later. "He always cautioned me that the mosquito monster would return some summer night—a night just like this—and begin its killing spree all over again."

I plop my body back down in my spot by the campfire and hold up my bottle of repellent. I shake it. "Bug spray?" I ask.

Everyone reaches out a hand, including Kenny.

3

I wake, and not a single nightmare haunted me during my sleep. I did dream about Neal's story though. The details of it have kind of stuck with me since he told it around the campfire two nights ago. But not in a frightening way. More like . . . curiosity.

Eh, it doesn't matter. I'm in my own bed now after spending half a week in the stink tent. It feels amazing. And on top of that, it's Saturday, my favorite day of the week.

I close my eyes and let the sun warm my face through the blinds, which I'm here for because the central air conditioning is set to arctic and is pumping through the vents. I could stay like this all day . . . but then my bedroom door creaks open.

I keep my eyes closed, pretending to still be asleep. I can feel my dad standing over my bed, and I silently wish to myself that he'll back his way out of my room. He always wants me to "seize the day" on the weekends, but what that really means is mowing the lawn, decluttering the basement, or cleaning out the gutters. After camping all week, I just want to have a lazy day inside with minimal to no sweating whatsoever.

The thing is, my dad doesn't leave. And he doesn't say anything either. He's just standing there, not even moving. I know because my floorboards are creaky and he's big enough to make each plank sing. He's an imposing guy—the kind who has to shop at specialty clothing stores otherwise all of his pants would come to a stop well above the ankle. With my nosiness growing, I choose to open one eye—just a bit—and take a peek. When I do, my dad, his dark skin looking like a shadow through my squinting eye, is staring down at me, holding my phone in his hand.

"It's my job to know when people are lying, you know that, right?" he asks like it is a question even though I'm clearly not supposed to answer.

Once a police officer, always a police officer.

I open both eyes, ending my acting career before it even begins. "It's not lying to pretend that you're sleeping."

"Mm-hmm," is all my dad says in response. He's too focused on rifling through my phone's settings to take the conversation any further.

"What are you doing with my phone?" I ask.

My dad stops what he's doing and glares down at me. "I'm making sure that your tracking app is activated so that I can keep tabs on you at all times."

I raise an eyebrow. "Did I do something wrong?"

Dad shakes his head and places my phone back down on the charging dock on my nightstand. "No, but if you did, I'd find out. Always remember that, Mr. Fake-Sleeper-to-Get-Out-of-Saturday-Chores. You're fooling no one. When you are really sleeping, there's a lot more drooling."

I sit up in bed and stretch my arms into the air. It feels so good that I let them linger up there until my shoulders get tired.

"You're being more of a police dad than usual," I say, expecting a laugh. None comes. Instead, my dad remains way too serious for a Saturday morning deep into summer vacation.

He wasn't always like this. I mean, he was always my dad, but after my mom disappeared a few years ago, he got a lot more protective. There was a time when he wouldn't even let me out of his sight at all. I understood it, but still, it was suffocating. Thankfully, those reins have loosened. At least, I thought they had.

"There's some stuff going on at work," he says hesitantly, rubbing at his eyes. Now that I'm sitting up, I realize he looks way more tired than he normally does. "I'd like you and your friends to stick to places where there are plenty of other people around and avoid going too far out—keep to the downtown area."

He looks down at my records, which I have housed in a series of overturned milk crates. He is familiar with almost every vinyl in the collection because most of them belonged to him at one time or another. And almost every single one of them features my mom's voice in some capacity or another.

She was a singer. And a really great one at that. She sang backup vocals with so many incredible artists. She toured the world. I mean, seriously, her life could have been a movie. But then she had me, and she decided to focus on being a mom. I am and will forever be grateful for that.

A few years ago, she decided to come out of retirement. She got an offer to go on tour with one of the biggest pop stars in the world. Her first instinct was to say no, but I actually convinced her to do it. She couldn't pass up an opportunity like that.

The thing is, she should have. I wish every day that she did because while she was on tour in Brazil, she disappeared. She was never seen or heard from again. Eventually, the Brazilian police declared her dead, but they never found her body.

Part of me likes to think that she's still out there and that she'll come home to Dad and me eventually.

Dad shifts his eyes from the record

collection to me again. "Anyway, you know what they say, it's better to be safe than to be sorry."

Once again, my nosiness has been piqued. "What kind of stuff are we talking about?"

This time, my dad does smile. And it's completely unexpected.

"The kind that we are not talking about," he says, turning away from my bed and heading for the door. "You don't have the clearance for that kind of information." He stops in the doorway and turns back to me. "Now I don't know what your day entails, but whatever it is, try to do it quietly. I worked an overnight and I need to get in a few hours of sleep because I pull another shift later this evening."

I flop back down onto my bed, letting my head sink into my pillow. "No problem there. You're witnessing my morning right now. After all that camping and hiking, I've been looking forward to a little rest and relaxation."

My dad nods. "You've got it—but tomorrow, that lawn needs to be mowed."

I grab hold of my pillow and bury my head

beneath it. The act of lazy defiance forces a chuckle from my dad. I hear him exit and close the door behind him.

4

I feel myself starting to drift off. There are moments when I can't tell if I'm awake or asleep. The sun continues to warm my face, but I've positioned myself in such a way that my eyes—even though closed—remain in the shadows. I feel cozy, like a caterpillar tucked away inside of its cocoon. Seriously, I wasn't kidding when I said that I could stay like this all day.

Suddenly, there's a surge of energy that surrounds my body. I convince myself that it's just my comforter, clinging to me in such a way that the friction is causing static to build up. The hairs on my arms stand on end and there's a tingling at the tip of my nose.

This all feels so familiar, and yet it has to be a dream, right? It couldn't be happening now. He couldn't be coming at this time.

I hear a faint *pop*, *pop*, *POP*, and then I feel what seems to be a sack of wet laundry drop down onto my stomach. The air is squashed out of my lungs, and I shoot upright, opening my eyes at the same time.

There, sitting on me, is an odd-looking creature that appears to be a cross between a prehistoric weasel and a modern-day llama. He is smiling.

At least, I think he is.

"Boo-en?" I whisper, swatting him off of me. "What are you doing here? Our agreement only extends to nights, not midday napping."

Boo-en is a paralysis demon. His particular breed of demon is known for slipping into bedrooms when people are sleeping and feeding on their energy. If you ever wake up feeling like you need a nap, chances are you've been visited by one of them.

Boo-en has been coming to see me for over a year now. He's like my own personal paralysis demon who keeps coming back for seconds because I, well, let him.

"My dad is just in the other room," I

continue. "You know that he doesn't have any idea about demons, and I really need to keep it that way. You being here in the daytime is going to make it a lot more difficult to keep quiet!"

Boo-en kneads at the comforter on my bed like a cat trying to get comfortable. "Damon not worry. Boo-en already checked on Damon's parental unit. Damon dad asleep."

I hunt demons, sure, but Boo-en is not one of those on my to-do list. He's more of an inside contact. He brings me information on other demons from time to time and even occasionally jumps in to save my tail. But mostly, our relationship is based on mutualism.

I learned that word—mutualism—in a book about the various kinds of relationships found in the animal and plant kingdoms. It means that both parties benefit from the relationship. An example would be pollination because both the bees and the flowers get something positive out of the deal.

Well, here's the thing. I actually never read that book, the one that I first learned about mutualism from. It was, however, read to me.

You see, some time ago, I heard that the human brain continues to learn while we're sleeping. Like, if I put a song on that I have never heard before and let it repeat all night, I'd wake up and consciously be able to recite the lyrics. That's pretty darn cool. Once I discovered that, I decided I wanted to make the most of my sleeping hours.

So when I met Boo-en, I proposed a pact: he can feed on my energy, but he has to read nonfiction books to me while he does. It works out quite well as long as I top off with an energy drink in the morning.

It helps that Boo-en prefers the company of humans over other demons. He also doesn't want to see our souls burn for all of eternity, which frankly makes him a lot more likable than most of the other demons I come across.

"Why would you come and visit now of all times?" I ask.

Boo-en finally sits, content with his kneading of the comforter. "Big bad demon in world with Damon. All demons talking about this."

I lean forward, my curiosity turning into concern. “There’s a big bad demon here, in Salem?”

Boo-en nods, which is a bit of a nauseating sight given his featherless turkey-like neck. He might be a good demon, but he is still difficult to look at sometimes. “Damon need be worried. This demon . . . more like god. Demon give life and take life away.”

“What kind of demon is it?” I ask.

Boo-en picks at his teeth, pulling a chunk of something free. He flicks it to my floor, and I make a mental note to vacuum my carpet as soon as he leaves.

“Boo-en not know. Boo-en ask around and no demon know. This demon always been in Salem. Salem is demon’s home. Demon sleeps for long time and wakes. That’s why so little known of demon.”

I don’t need to hear the rest to know why Boo-en made a special trip here to warn me. “And now it’s awake again,” I say with certainty.

Boo-en nods again. I’m thankful for not having had breakfast yet. I don’t think I could keep it all down.

"But Damon should know . . . Damon dad too close to demon. Damon dad work put Damon dad on path with demon. Boo-en worried Damon dad to be next victim."

5

After a quick vacuuming of my bedroom carpet, I creep through the house to my dad's room and peer inside.

He's asleep. Perfect. If what Boo-en says is true, I need to do some serious snooping around in order to find out how my dad is crossing paths with a godlike demon.

For starters, demon knowledge is not common knowledge. Other than Liam, Madelyn, and myself, no one in my circle knows of their existence. In fact, I bet if you took a poll of Salem's population, more people would believe in the tooth fairy than buy into the fact that demons are walking the streets among us. (We actually once fought a demon that was pretending to be the tooth fairy so it could collect human teeth as part of its own personal collection. That was a troubling case.)

My dad is the last person on the planet I'd want to know about my demon hunting. He'd flip a literal lid if he was wearing a hat when he found out. There is no way he'd ever want me putting myself in that kind of danger. He wouldn't even sit down and talk about it with me. He'd just ground me until I was old and gray.

Talking isn't my dad's strong suit. Especially when it comes to feelings. He can be a bit of a closed book with that kind of stuff. Even after my mom disappeared, as much as he was there for me, he never really let anyone be there for him. He dealt with her disappearance and the authorities declaring her dead in the exact same way he does with everything difficult that he has ever faced—by working through it on his own.

Anyway, I know my dad. If his work has crossed over into mine, the evidence will be available in his duffel bag that he takes to the precinct every day. For whatever reason, he thinks the zipper on that bag is like a magical lock that will keep everyone but him out. I'm sure it just doesn't even occur to him that anyone would nose around inside of it, especially me. I almost feel guilty about breaking that unspoken trust.

Almost.

I find the duffel bag sitting on one of the chairs in the dining room. I unzip it slowly. A gush of foul gym sock air wafts out and assaults my nose. I press forward, spreading the two sides of the bag apart and peering inside. There's the usual list of suspects—a crumpled bag of unopened crackers, a metallic badge issued to him from the city, and the gym socks responsible for the foul smell. But there's also something that catches my eye: a manila folder.

I look back over my shoulder, making sure that my dad hasn't snuck up on me. Instead, I pick up the familiar sound of snoring coming from his bedroom at the end of the hallway. He's still asleep.

I slip the manila folder out of the duffel bag and place it on the dining room table. I take a deep breath and then open it.

A stack of paperwork stares back at me.

Police reports. Personal notes. Crime scene photos. And they're all beyond disturbing and oddly familiar at the same time.

I scan through the reports. The names of the victims don't ring any bells, but the dates of the crimes do. Both of them happened while I was away on my camping trip.

I hear a creak that causes my body to stiffen. Could it be my dad?

I don't move as I wait and listen for follow-up footsteps. None come. It must have just been the house settling.

I return my eyes to the troubling stack of paperwork. Two deaths and they were both deemed "mysterious" by the investigating detectives. That's strange.

I dig further into the reports, looking for a cause of death. What I find makes my heart skip a beat.

By the looks of it, both people had all of the blood removed from their bodies. Their brains were also missing. But that is way too much of a coincidence. It's the exact same way that the victims died in Neal's campfire tale.

Hmm. I suppose Neal *could* have known about these deaths and crafted his story around them. That would make sense.

I keep digging through the pile of paperwork and come across some ancient, yellowed files dated from the 1950s. The oldest one in the stack references an "unspecified animal attack" that happened alongside a road out by the swampland. The victim was a businessperson from out of town.

Nope. Definitely can't be a coincidence. Neal's story has to be true. But that would mean . . .

"There really is a mosquito man," I say quietly to myself.

I'm going to need to make a much bigger batch of my homemade bug spray.

I call an emergency meeting of the demon hunting squad to go over what Boo-en told me and the additional information I pulled from my dad's work folder. As far as I can tell, we've got a demon on the loose who may or may not be the one mentioned in Neal's campfire tale. Either way, whatever is stalking Salem, someone needs to take care of it before anyone else gets hurt.

Like my dad.

I arrive at the public library about ten minutes before our scheduled meeting time. I spot a familiar cat licking up a fallen ice cream cone in the parking lot. I'm actually surprised that I'm not the first one on the scene.

We agreed to use the gazebo out in front of the library as our office today. The heat today is so oppressive that I struggle to breathe comfortably with all of the humidity in the air. I pass the time waiting for everyone to show up by staring out at the abandoned single-screen movie theater across the street and sweating until my clothes are damp.

The old Marquee theater across the street was the hot spot in my grandpa's day. It was alive and kicking when the first victim showed up on the side of the road by the swamp. I wonder why Grandpa never mentioned any of that mosquito man business to me? Maybe he just didn't want to scare me. If he only knew the kinds of things I've seen and heard since then. His mind would be blown.

It's hard to believe that so much has come and gone since that first "unspecified animal attack." It makes me so mad that such evil has outlived so much and so many people.

Always punctual, Madelyn is the first to arrive. I spot her purple umbrella bopping up and down the street before I see her. It's not raining, but Madelyn still needs the umbrella. She was born with albinism, so it's super important that she keep herself out of the sun as much as possible. That's why we're in the gazebo—it provides a good bit of shade while still being outdoors.

"Hey, Damon," Madelyn says, skipping up the steps to the gazebo. Her white-blond hair bounces like a fleeing rabbit as she ascends the steps, giving her more height. This is of great benefit to Madelyn because height is an area that she hasn't been blessed in. "How was the camping trip?"

I shrug my shoulders. "As good as could be expected in this heat."

Madelyn turns her umbrella over and rests it on its head. "You New Englanders are such babies when the temperatures start rising."

Madelyn is originally from Texas. Her family moved here a few years ago, hoping that the relatively dank weather of Salem would lead to fewer days of being exposed to the sun. Even though she can't always enjoy it, Madelyn absolutely loves this kind of heat. She would be perfectly happy living in the desert.

And she's not the only one.

"If you think the Lone Star State is hot, try

spending a weekend in The Pit," Liam says as he saunters into view from around the corner of the library. "Now *they* know how to turn up the thermostat."

Liam is the biggest kid in our school. He has had to continuously turn down the recruitment attempts of both the football coach and the hockey coach. He's as solid as a refrigerator and, if you asked him, twice as cool as one.

His aura also looks much different than Madelyn's. In fact, it looks much different than any other human's. That's because he's not actually a human. He's a trickster demon.

I know how that sounds. I hunt demons and my best friend *is* one? I'll admit, I never expected to bond with a demon. But I can say without a doubt that Liam is a genuinely good dude. I knew it as soon as I saw him, too.

His aura is a twisting knot of darkness and despair, sure, but there's more to it than that. Deep within it is the faintest hint of color. It's an inner orange glow that I call his aura's heart. This is not common with demon auras, and it speaks to Liam's humanlike empathy. Just because he was born in the darkness doesn't mean that he has to embrace it.

"I could still handle it better than Damon can handle a Salem summer," Madelyn says, referring back to the heat in The Pit.

"I have a poor internal cooling system," I declare in self-defense. "Besides, I didn't call us all here today so you two could make fun of me."

"And yet still we are," Liam says with a smile as he climbs up the stairs into the gazebo.

Being a trickster, Liam never passes up an opportunity to poke fun. It's as natural to him as breathing.

"Hold the phone, Daddy-O," Ricky says as the cat leaps onto the railing of the gazebo. There is still ice cream smearing the fur around its mouth. "Did we miss a big tickle at Damon's expense?"

"Who invited the frustrating feline?" Liam asks with his nose turned up in the air.

"I did," I say. "We need their help."

Ricky and his better half Denise were once

teenage boyfriend and girlfriend. They had grown up in Salem and started officially dating during their junior year of high school. That was in 1956.

Unfortunately for everyone, Ricky was into drag racing, and he got challenged one night by his archnemesis, a boy who apparently wore a pair of 3D glasses from the Marquee all the time because he thought they were cool. After accepting the challenge, Ricky was on his way to winning the race, but then something happened that he couldn't have planned for. A cat ran out in the street in front of his car, and the car crashed. Denise was in the passenger seat when it happened. They both died instantly. Their souls have been bound together inside of that cat ever since.

The weird part is that each of their souls represents a different section of the feline's evenly divided body. Here, let me help paint the picture a little better. Physically, one side of the cat has black fur, which is where Ricky resides, and the other side of the cat has white fur, which is where Denise is bound.

Therefore, when Ricky speaks, it's out of the left side of the cat's mouth. For Denise, it's the right side.

It also helps that Denise talks more like the rest of us. Ricky sounds like some greaser extra from a teen drama set during the 1950s. Sure, it's all very weird, but by now we all kind of just go with it.

"Kindness," Denise reminds her boyfriend. "Damon is our friend, remember?"

I nod at the cat, thankful for Denise's support. "I also feed you, Ricky," I add. "Let's not forget that, either."

Ricky stands down, as do the rest of my friends. With playtime now over, we get right to work.

7

The meeting goes smoothly, and everyone is on board with pooling our resources and doing what we can to stop the mosquito man from claiming any more victims.

Ricky is always a bit reluctant to get his paws dirty, so I promise to hand over an extra can of tuna for Denise and him once we solve the case. He makes me agree to buy them solid white albacore instead of the usual chunk light variety.

It's a small price to pay for his cooperation.

"So, to summarize," I say, going over the plan once again so that we all know our roles. "Ricky and Denise can travel where the rest of us can't. They'll hit the alleyways and windowsills, listening in for any information that may help us.

"Righty-O, Daddy-O."

“Madelyn will head into the library and do some research on the previous attacks. Whatever happened in the past will help us solve what’s going on in the present. At least, that’s the hope.”

“I’ve got some good ideas about where to start looking,” Madelyn adds before I continue.

“And Liam and I will go over to Neal’s house and see if we can gather any more information from him relating to his grandfather’s story. There may have been a detail or two that he left out or that I missed because I was wrestling with that nightmare demon.”

Everyone nods in agreement and breaks away from the gazebo, turning the plan into action.

“But wait,” I announce, stopping everyone before we go our separate ways. “Remember that my dad is working this same case. We have to be careful, and most importantly, we have to catch this thing before it hurts him. Boo-en said he’s already gotten too close, and I can't have anything happen to my dad."

I say my piece. Everyone knows how important this is. Ricky and Denise disappear into the bushes and skulk away. Madelyn enters the library and begins her research.

"I think there's something you're missing in this plan of yours, pal," Liam says to me as we make our way to our discarded bikes on the side of the library. "Neal told this story. He knew about all of those details. He could be the demon."

I actually hadn't thought about that. I suppose it's possible, but I've known him since I was just a Hatchling. "I haven't seen anything in his aura that would suggest that he would be."

Liam grabs the handles of his bike and lifts it up so it's upright on its tires. "His grandfather then."

I don't like being unprepared. I also don't like surprises. If either is possible—the demon hiding out in Neal or his grandfather—I'd certainly rather know ahead of time.

I nod as I climb onto my bike. "We'll make a special stop on the way to Neal's house. Just in case."

Neal's family lives on the outskirts of town where some of the last farms in Salem still exist. Liam knows where his house is because he went on a date with Neal's older sister at the end of the school year. Let's just say that it wasn't a romance that withstood the test of time like Ricky and Denise.

"She told me I was immature and infantile," Liam said after the date went south. I didn't have the heart to tell him that she pretty much summed up a trickster demon perfectly.

After a brief pit stop at the local dollar store, it takes Liam and me about twenty minutes to make it out to Neal's place. I hope my dad's still sleeping because if he tracks my whereabouts through my phone, I'm going to have a difficult time explaining why I gave up a comfortable bed for a cornfield in the scorching hot sun.

We wait in the field across the street from Neal's house, making sure his parents aren't home. There are no cars in the driveway, but that could mean a lot of things. After about a half hour of standing in the corn and picking ticks off of our legs, we decide to make our move.

"Are we sure there isn't a . . . cleaner way to do this?" I ask.

Liam starts to trudge out of the field toward the street. "You said it yourself; it's possible that he could disguise his aura. This is the only way to be sure."

"But wouldn't that make his sister a demon, too?" I point out as I follow Liam out of the field.

"Well, she did call me infantile," Liam says with a pained expression as he looks both ways to make sure that the street is safe for crossing. "That alone is suspect behavior."

It's really not, but I don't say that to Liam. Instead, we cross the street and step into Neal's front yard. I reach into the pocket of my shorts and pull out a tiny transparent squirt gun that we picked up on the way over. It's currently filled with holy water. Just in case.

"I'll stay out of sight to start," Liam says, pushing me up the steps to the front porch. "If he changes into your mosquito man, I'll swoop in, ready to swat the big bug down!"

Liam is a great best friend, but he's also a pretty awesome demon hunting partner. Because he's a demon himself, he's incredibly strong, which makes him the tank of our squad. I once saw him rip an entire tree out of the ground just because it was infested with spongy moth larvae and he didn't want them to spread to the other trees and take over the entire forest.

It was both impressive and, if I'm being honest, a bit heartwarming. Who goes to those kinds of lengths to save a bunch of trees?

I step up to the front door as Liam ducks behind a porch swing.

I consider knocking but opt for ringing the doorbell instead. I don't want to have one of those awkward moments where you're wondering if anyone actually heard the knock so you then have to decide if you should knock again. Moments like that keep me up at night. Sometimes, it's just easier to remove any second-guessing from the mission before it has a chance to make an appearance.

After a few seconds, I hear the door handle of the old barn-style door jangle on the other side. It opens, and Neal is now standing in the doorway. He looks confused.

"Damon?" he asks, surely surprised to find one of his fellow Chickadees standing on his front porch.

Without saying a word, I raise the squirter to chest level and unleash a stream of holy water all over Neal's arms. If he isn't human, this will do a number on him, just like it did that pesky nightmare demon.

Neal's exposed flesh doesn't begin to bubble and blacken like the nightmare demon's, though. He doesn't let loose a bloodcurdling screech upon being drenched in the liquid. And he certainly doesn't dissolve into a mound of shaving-cream-like goo. Instead, he just stares out at me with a look of absolute confusion, now wetter than he was before opening the door.

His aura is about thirty different shades of blue and is shaped like a hot-air balloon caught in a powerful gust of wind. The colors remain vibrant even after the holy water exposure.

Neal is not a demon.

"We have to talk," I say to him, lowering the squirter.

8

Liam runs full speed and does a cannonball onto Neal's bed, knocking the headboard into the wall.

"Are either of you going to actually tell me what this is all about?" Neal asks.

Liam flips over from his back to his belly, coming to a standstill on Neal's springy mattress.

"Can you tell us more about that story of your grandfather's that you told at the campout? We just need to know if there are any additional details."

"How come?"

"Just tell us," Liam urges. "Then we'll decide how much you should know after that."

Neal scowls and reluctantly steps up to his bed. He avoids eye contact with Liam as he kneels down and pulls out a large, flat box from beneath the bed. He slides it across the floor to the center of the room and opens it. Inside is a collection of mementos and keepsakes from Neal's grandfather, who he tells us died a few years ago.

I stand over the box looking into it. Liam leaps off of the bed and joins me in my gawking.

Neal digs through the contents of the box and removes a black spiral-bound journal. He steps back, collapsing into a large bright red beanbag chair. The chair lets out a puff of air as it accepts Neal's body. He opens the journal and then flips through the pages until he finds what he is looking for.

"This first one is dated August 31, 1956," he says, looking down at the cursive writing in the journal. "My grandfather lived in Tennessee for a few years before he moved back to Salem, so he writes with a bit of twang in here. Anyway, the entry says, 'I don't know what it is that I saw but I know it ain't natural. It must be what's out there doing all that killing. I tried to tell my mom about it, but she looked at me like I had ten heads. That told me all I needed to know about saying anything to anyone else about it.'"

"How old was your grandfather at the time when he wrote this?" I ask.

Neal shrugs, causing him to sink even farther into the beanbag chair. "I guess about our age. Maybe a bit older."

I nod. Neal continues reading from the entry in the journal.

"'I've kept my mouth closed since. I still need to vent about it though. I suppose this journal is better than nothing. The face of the thing still haunts me. Its eyes came out of the side of its head, looking like half grapefruits with hundreds of lenses covering each one. It didn't have a nose or a mouth as far as I could see. Instead, it had this thing sticking out of its face like an elephant's trunk, only shorter. The trunk thing flicked at the air in my direction, and I swear it was smelling me with it. I started to pray. I knew I was as good as dead. But that creature, for whatever reason, turned around and walked right into the swamp and disappeared into the water. The spot it went in was the same fishing hole the hornpout calls its home. I dropped my pole and gear box and ran out of there as fast as I could.'"

Liam kneels down and begins to dig through the contents of the box himself. "Am I the only one who doesn't know what a hornpout is?"

"It's a type of catfish," Neal says. "He used to like fishing for them because they give a good fight."

"Was that the last mention of the mosquito man in the journal?" I ask, hoping to keep us on track.

Neal shakes his head. "No. There's a few more. The next one is dated September 15, 1956. It says, 'I think I'm cursed. I ain't slept much at all since I saw that creature out in the swamp. I try to forget about it, but it doesn't seem to forget me. I see its face every time I close my eyes. On top of it all, I . . . I ain't ever going to forgive myself neither. I thought a drag race would help get my mind off of what I saw. I thought it would help me outrun the nightmares somehow. But there was an accident. The other driver and his girl . . . they didn't make it.'"

Liam reaches down into the box of things and pulls out an old pair of paper 3D glasses with the name of the Marquee written along the side. Liam holds up the glasses so that I can see them, and his eyes go wide. He has connected the same set of dots that I have. Neal's grandfather was the person who challenged Ricky to the drag race all those years ago that led to Denise and him being stuck in a cat.

I shake my head, telling Liam without words that now is not the time to talk about that *particular* detail from the journal.

"This is the last one about the creature," Neal continues, not picking up on our discovery. "It's dated September 22, 1956. It says, 'I started doing research and I think I know what I saw. I talked to an old-timer who has more stories than a library. He seemed to recognize exactly what I was describing. He said that there was once a demon so powerful that early settlers feared the lands that are now Salem and the neighboring communities. Eventually the demon clashed with the people and they managed to defeat it, but it promised to return and feast on those who took its land from it. The settlers burned the creature, and its ash became what we know as mosquitoes. Now its millions upon millions of offspring collect the blood of people to build the creature's strength back up so that it can return to feast for yet another season.'"

Neal closes the journal.

"That's it?" I ask, just to be sure.

"It doesn't come up again in any of his writing. I've read the journal dozens of times." He pauses. "Now are you both going to finally tell me what this is all about?"

I tell Neal everything that we know about the recent deaths highlighted in my dad's reports—how the victim's bodies were drained of blood and how they were both missing their brains. Each detail that lines up with Neal's campfire tale causes his face to twitch.

"So, you're telling me this monster is real just like grandfather said it was?" Neal asks, landing somewhere between surprise and I told you so.

I turn away from the box and take Neal in. His long body hangs off of every inch of the beanbag chair. "It's too much of a coincidence for these new victims to be turning up in the same exact way, especially knowing that your grandfather was so concerned that the demon would eventually come back. If it's not real, then someone is going to some pretty extreme lengths to make us think that it is."

Neal's head cocks to one side. "And you thought I could have been the monster?"

"Really more of a demon like your grandfather wrote about in his journal," Liam says, dropping the paper 3D glasses down into the box. "And you can never be too careful. We've seen all sorts of stuff, so we at least had to check."

Neal tries to get out of the beanbag chair, but any shift in his weight causes him to sink farther into it. He has to flop off like a fish and then pick himself up off of the floor instead.

"That's the part of all of this that's most confusing to me," he says as he stands upright. "How do you know about all this stuff?"

Liam and I look at each other, unsure how to answer the question. We don't make it a habit of telling people about our demon hunting. Most of what we do, we do in secret. Before I can nominate Liam to summarize things for Neal, he touches the side of his nose with his index finger, signaling "not it." And because Liam beat me to it, that means the summary falls solely on me now.

I choose to keep things mysterious and opt for a page out of my dad's playbook. "Sorry, Neal. How we know is classified and you don't have the clearance." Liam grins. "We just want to stop it, so we're thankful for the information that you provided. And I apologize for squirting you with the holy water."

Neal steps forward. A look of determination washes over him. "I'm going to help you guys track it down."

Liam laughs and then pats Neal on the back. "That's a good one, kid, but my suggestion is that you leave the demon hunting to the professionals."

Neal swats Liam's hand aside defiantly. "First of all, I'm not okay with you calling me a kid. Last I checked, we were the same age."

"Actually—"

I glare at Liam, stopping him before he says anything else. Neal doesn't need to know that Liam is over two hundred years old, which is basically a teenager in demon years.

"And secondly," Neal continues, "I'm the

best tracker of all of the Chickadees. Just ask Damon. He'll tell you."

I nod. He's right about that. He's won the top badge in tracking three years in a row. That's no easy feat.

"And thirdly?" Liam asks snidely, now fully annoyed by Neal pushing his way into our investigation.

Neal looks right into Liam's eyes. "Thirdly, this was my grandfather's burden. He carried it with him his whole life. If anyone should stop this demon thing, it's me. Or at least, I should be a part of it. I owe my grandfather that."

I turn to Liam and shrug my shoulders. "I mean, it does put a nice bow on the whole package, don't you think?"

Liam sighs.

"Plus, he really *is* a great tracker."

Liam throws his hands up in surrender. "Fine! The little bird scout can tag along." He points a finger at Neal. "But you'd better stay out of my way!"

Liam storms out of Neal's bedroom, kicking aside the beanbag chair as he does.

I smile uncomfortably at Neal, who seems a bit taken aback by the unexpected tantrum. "Don't worry, once he warms up to you, Liam becomes way more—"

"Friendly?" Neal asks, hopeful.

My smiles fades. "Let's go with tolerable."

10

Liam, Neal, and I ride our bikes out to Lickity Splits, a roadside ice cream stand that butts up against the highway. Seventy years ago, this was prime swamp real estate. Today, only a few acres of swamp remain, and it's now protected land. Unless someone changes a few laws, it will stay undeveloped for the foreseeable future.

I went ahead and shut off the tracker app on my phone before we left Neal's house. I know that this is a risky endeavor, but I'd rather fib about it not working properly than have to explain to my dad why I'm out at the epicenter of his suspicious death investigation. I'll get in trouble either way, but this is the lesser of two punishments.

"Are we sure this is even the place?" Liam asks, resting his bike against the side of the shack-like building. Sweetness hangs in the air, a combination of waffle cones and rainbow sprinkles.

"I'm sure," Neal responds, dropping his bike down onto the gravel that seconds as the Lickity Splits parking lot. "My grandfather used to take me out for ice cream here every weekend. He said when he was a kid, this was just an empty lot by the side of the road. It's where he parked that morning to go fishing. Then he crossed the street and entered the swamp right over there."

Neal points across the street to an area of overgrown shrubs, weeds, and thorn bushes. If there's a path behind that scattering of lush summer foliage, it's well-hidden.

I look down at my watch. "Well, Madelyn was catching the bus from the library, so she should be here in a few minutes. I guess we can just wait until then and see what she has learned. We can come up with a plan once we're all together."

To pass the time, we each get a cone of ice cream from the take-out window. I recognize the girl who takes our order as Lola, an incoming senior at Salem High School. She doesn't seem to place Liam and me—or she just doesn't care—but she does acknowledge Neal.

"Hey," she says to Neal, jotting our orders down on a tiny pad of paper. "How's your sister enjoying her summer?"

Neal shrugs. "Good, I guess. She's working at the grocery store. I haven't seen her a lot."

Lola nods knowingly. "I hear that. I've been standing in this window all summer, too." She looks down at her pad and then back up at Liam. "Is this serious? You want *six* scoops of peppermint?"

Liam rests his elbow on the window and leans in toward Lola, smiling flirtatiously. "I never kid about ice cream."

"Umm, whatever," Lola says, sneering at Liam's awkward flirtation. "I'll go get your orders."

As Lola disappears from the window, Neal turns away and shakes his head. "Well, that was embarrassing. I can't believe my sister ever agreed to go on a date with you."

If there's one thing I know about Liam,

it's that he doesn't like to be mocked by just anyone. To him, you have to earn the right to jab and jest, and Neal hasn't earned anything yet. Liam is the true definition of someone who can dish it and not take it.

Liam steps right into Neal's personal space until their noses are basically touching. His eyes glow a bitter, piercing yellow, which causes a visceral, fear-based reaction out of Neal. "I'm happy to show you just how 'infantile' I can be, bird scout."

Neal backs away from Liam, pointing at him as he does. "Your eyes . . . they just . . . changed!"

I grab hold of Neal and pull him off to the side of the building. I holler back at Liam. "Way to go! Now you're paying for all of our ice cream!"

As Liam waits for our orders to be scooped, I try to calm Neal down. It doesn't go well.

"He's one of them! Liam is a monster!"

I shake my head emphatically, mostly so that Neal's eyes will focus on me and not Liam. "No. He's not a monster. He's a trickster demon, but he's not bad. He helps hunt demons who want to do terrible things—like this mosquito man we're after. Liam just has a difficult time letting new people into the fold, you know?"

Neal's eyes are as wide as saucers.

"Please, I need you to trust me, Neal," I say to him. "We're both Chickadee Scouts, right? Well, what's the first rule we're taught as Hatchlings?"

Neal seems to break from his trance. He answers the question, but it's like his brain is on autopilot. "A Chickadee must be able to count on his flock at all times."

I nod. "That's right. And you can count on me because I'm a part of that flock. Liam is a good guy. Actually, he's the *best* guy. And he's going to help us give your grandfather's memory some closure."

Whatever I said seems to have worked. Neal's lanky body becomes less tense, and his expression softens. Behind me, I hear the unmistakable squeaking of bus brakes as one pulls slowly into the Lickity Splits lot, its massive tires crushing the gravel beneath its weight.

Liam arrives from around the corner, carrying three cones of ice cream, one stacked six scoops high. He hands me mine—peanut butter crunch—and then passes Neal his—black raspberry. Liam looks regretful.

"Listen," he says, not so much looking at Neal as looking past him, "I'm sorry. I shouldn't have scared you like that. It's not how I like to be, you know? It's not easy being a demon in a human world, especially when you'd prefer to just be like . . . well, everybody else."

Wow. That's some serious growth from Liam. I'm impressed, but not as impressed as Neal is when Liam detaches his jaw and swallows all six scoops of his ice cream in one gulp. (Fun fact: Those people who win the hot dog eating competition every Fourth of July—*all* trickster demons!)

With one problem now seemingly resolved, we turn our attention to the idling bus as its door opens. Madelyn, wearing a flowery straw sun hat that casts her entire self in shadow, steps down off of the bus. She's holding a cat carrier. Inside the carrier are Ricky and Denise.

"Madelyn, I'm sure you know Neal," I say as she approaches us.

She nods. "We have gym together."

"You're not a demon too, are you?" he asks, not entirely comfortable.

Madelyn shakes her head. "Nope. Just a regular old human."

"Why does this square look so familiar?" I hear Ricky's voice ask from inside the confines of the cat carrier. Liam and I glance in each other's direction, realizing at the same time that Neal must look a lot like his grandfather.

Once again, Neal's eyes become saucers. He squats down and directs his eyes on the multicolored cat inside the carrier. "Di . . . did your cat just talk?"

"They're not a regular old cat," Madelyn says as she places the carrier down on the gravel. She opens the door and out steps Ricky and Denise, their eyes plastered on Neal's face. "They're actually a couple of spirits trapped in a cat's body, which I now realize sounds pretty ridiculous as I say it out loud."

Neal stares down at the cat. Ricky and Denise stare up at Neal.

"Oh, that reminds me," Liam says with a soft giggle, interrupting the gawk session, "I think if you put these on it will really help, Neal."

Liam reaches into his pocket and pulls out the pair of 3D glasses. He hands them to Neal.

"Are these my grandfather's?" he asks.

"Sure are. And I didn't steal them. I just borrowed them because I anticipated this exact moment happening and I knew it was one that I couldn't possibly pass up."

Before I can reach out and stop Neal from putting on the glasses, they're already on his face. A look of recognition washes over Ricky and Denise, and they let out a hiss that startles all of us except for Liam. The cat lunges at Neal, claws exposed.

11

"It was just one scratch," Liam says as he leads the group through the thorn bushes, holding the branches aside so that we can all pass unscathed. "I grabbed the cat before they went and did any real damage."

"It was still a cruel prank," I tell him, making sure that Neal can hear me.

I want him to know that he can still trust me. A Chickadee must be able to count on his flock, after all.

"You had just gotten done apologizing to him. It was unnecessary."

Liam's feet splash down into a section of saturated ground. The transition to swamp has begun. "I'll admit that the timing wasn't ideal, but I'm a trickster. What do you want from me?"

Ricky and Denise release a low, guttural

growl from their throat. It's aimed at Liam.

"Those 3D shades brought it all into focus for us, Daddy-O," Ricky says to Neal as he and Denise tiptoe through the soggy soil. Just like most cats, these two aren't fans of getting wet. "You literally looked like your grandfather when he was sitting there in his chariot, ready to punch the gas and take off from the line. I'm sorry we flipped our lid."

Neal rubs at the fresh scratch on his cheek. "He never forgave himself for what happened. My grandfather would never knowingly hurt anyone. He wasn't that kind of person. It was the mosquito man. That thing consumed his thoughts, and I think it broke him down emotionally."

Neal is talking to Ricky and Denise casually. All things considered, I think he's handling this entire thing really well. Not many people could carry on a conversation with two spirits trapped in a cat that just attacked them and adjust to it being a normal way of life this quickly. I'm impressed.

Using their claws, Ricky and Denise

climb up the trunk of a nearby tree and travel along on a branch, balancing like an acrobat as they pass over a particularly deep area of swamp water.

The cat speaks out of the right side of its mouth, which means Denise is talking. "We've had a lot of time to process what happened that night. We don't blame your grandfather. If anything, we blame ourselves."

The cat continues to speak, but the words now come from the left side of its mouth. "Bingo. Drag racing was my bag, Daddy-O. I was always out cruisin' for a bruisin' because I looked for trouble even when it wasn't looking for me. I'm just sorry—and forever will be—that my best girl in the whole wide world was with me when it finally caught up with me."

We walk in silence for a bit, everyone internalizing their own thoughts. I can't help but think that there's a big picture component going on here that we're just not seeing yet.

I look up at the sky through the canopy of trees. It's almost dusk.

"Did you find anything in your research

that could help us, Madelyn?" I ask, breaking the silence.

Madelyn pulls out her phone and looks down at the screen. "I found a lot, but I'm still not sure how any of it is going to help us. I fed all of the information I pulled from old records into an artificial intelligence program I created. It's analyzing everything, searching the web for any corresponding data that could prove any possible connections between the past and the present. What I can say is that the sightings of the mosquito man go back much further than the 1950s."

"How much further?" Neal asks.

Madelyn lowers her phone. From this angle, I can see the screen says 53 percent of the data analyzing is complete. "Centuries."

"We weren't able to turn up much else on our end either," Denise adds. "There is some spirit chatter going around about the demon, but none of those lingering souls tend to believe anything can be done about it. They seem to think that it's inevitable that the demon goes away and eventually returns. It's not so much an event as it is a process."

I've been thinking a lot about the journal passages that Neal's grandfather wrote. Let's just say for the sake of argument that his research was accurate and that all the mosquitoes in the world are each a small piece of the demon.

How can we kill it without killing every single mosquito? That would be impossible, so does that mean that killing the demon itself is impossible, too?

What if all we can do is just weaken it enough to send it back into hibernation early? Will that be enough to keep my dad safe?

No sooner do I complete my thought than the distant din of thousands upon thousands of vibrating wings fills the thick, heavy air. It's like a cloud of sound has moved in over the swamp, creating an all-consuming thunder of buzzing.

Without hearing what he heard back in 1956, I can only assume that this is the same sound Neal's grandfather wrote about in his journal.

It's got to be the swarm of mosquitoes that was said to surround the demon.

"Anybody bring the insect repellent?" Liam asks.

12

Madelyn looks down at her phone. "The mosquito man data is still running through my program. It's up to 67 percent. I need more time to access the results."

Liam punches his fist into his open hand, emphasizing his tough guy persona. "Ask and you shall receive, my friend."

"We have to find it before you can punch it, Liam," I say. "Let's split up into pairs so we can cover as much ground as possible. Neal, you come with me. We'll head to the west. Liam and Madelyn, you two go straight ahead. Ricky and Denise, you take the east."

"Why don't we get one of you squares to go with and keep us company?" Ricky asks as he licks at his paw and then rubs it up against his face.

"Because he said 'pairs' and there's two of

you in there already," Liam says, marching forward with Madelyn. "Now do your part and don't engage if you find it."

I nod in agreement. "That goes for everyone. No one attack this thing alone. It's too dangerous and we don't know what it's capable of."

"Lucky for me then that I'm going out there with the biggest brainiac in the bunch," Liam says with a chuckle. "If it's hungry for brains, Madelyn will definitely be its first choice."

Madelyn rolls her eyes. "And even luckier for you then because you have no brain at all, so what would it be able to eat?" She looks down at her phone again. "Seventy-one percent now—the final stretch. Let's just hope we can survive the last twenty-nine."

We wish each other good luck and then head off in our separate directions. Neal and I forge a path to the left. The ground quickly becomes flooded with standing water. My feet sink into the choking mud, releasing the fetid stench of decaying organic matter. Frogs leap away and centipedes skitter off. The daylight continues to fade.

I'm sure Dad is wondering where I am. By now he'll be checking the unresponsive tracking app and devising my punishment.

"Your dad's a cop, right, Damon?" Neal asks. His voice cuts through the constant buzzing of mosquitoes, which seems to be coming from all around us now.

"He is," I answer, nearly losing my shoe to the muck. Every step I take causes a vacuum beneath the mud, and the earth practically eats my foot whole. It's getting increasingly difficult to keep my balance.

"Can't you just have him handle all of this mosquito man business?"

I shake my head, not knowing if Neal can see the action in the diminishing light. "The police are not equipped to handle a situation like this. Their batons and bullets wouldn't do a thing. I'd imagine my dad and his coworkers would have the same reaction to learning that demons exist that you did. People are just not prepared to see the world in this way, and I don't blame them. I think I had the benefit of being so young when I learned the truth. I didn't know differently, you know? I had nothing to compare it against."

I hear the mud squishing into Neal's shoes and then the powerful suction sound of him pulling each foot out again. We're both going to need a serious shower and deodorizing when we get out of this swamp.

Assuming that we do ever get out of this swamp.

"That must have been so hard," he says between two sloshing steps. "You had to carry this on your own for all these years. That's a lot."

I shrug, not wanting to take too much credit for the only reality I've ever known. "I had Liam and Madelyn. We are always there for each other because we know we aren't living normal lives. We've always been aware of that and we're each other's biggest support system because of it. Your grandfather, though, he had to work through the truth about demons all on his own. Now him I feel for."

Neal doesn't have a chance to respond.

Instead, a sharp, high-pitched scream rips through the swamp, causing goosebumps to ripple over my exposed skin. At first, I think the scream might be human, but on the second burst of sound, I recognize it for what it is—a deer bleat, the sound the animals are known to make when they're in grave danger.

I run ahead, rushing toward the panicked screams of the animal before they fade away. I know Neal is on my tail because I can hear him struggling to wade through the sludge just below the surface of the swamp water. I push my way through a closely packed thicket of thorn bushes, cutting my legs and arms up and leaving my own DNA evidence behind for my dad to use against me in the looming case of my forever grounding.

I emerge on the other side of the angry bushes, and it's as if a fog now hangs over the swamp. I realize quickly that this fog is alive, though. It's the scourge of mosquitoes, and there, at the center of the cloud, I see it. About twenty yards away from where I'm standing is the mosquito man.

It's big. Too big for me to pat the top of its head, even if I were standing on my tippy toes. Not that I would want to.

It's definitely more mosquito than man, at least in terms of its features. Its skin is dark brown, a shade or two darker than mine, and speckled with black spots. Wisps of white highlight its limbs, almost like tiger stripes. The terrifying creature somehow looks fragile and strong at the same time. And its eyes—those terribly inhuman eyes—are spheres of wild incomprehension.

The mosquito man is hunched over a now lifeless white-tailed deer, its monstrous *proboscis*—a term I picked up from Boo-en reading *The Anatomy of Insects* to me a few months back—is drinking from the animal's neck, emptying it of its blood—every last life-giving drop.

"It was all true," Neal says in awe as he emerges from the thorn bushes and sees firsthand the demon that had haunted his grandfather. "The mosquito man is real!"

The creature looks up at us, acknowledging

our arrival, and then lets out an ear-piercing shriek that causes my toes to curl. It may have allowed Neal's grandfather to walk away without harming him, but that's not the vibe it's giving me right now.

"Run!" I scream as the demon drops the mummified corpse of the deer into the brackish water and leaps in our direction.

13

Because of the mud anchoring me in place, I'm unable to escape the creature's attack in time. With the height and frame of a professional basketball player, it feels like a freight train hitting me. I'm uprooted from the mud—literally knocked out of my shoes—and sent hurtling into the thorn bushes.

My head spins, and I have a hard time catching my breath. I've had the wind completely knocked out of me.

"Damon?" I hear Liam's concerned voice say, but it seems like it's a million miles away.

It takes a moment for me to realize that my entire backside is now a pin cushion for thorns. I want to peel myself off of the branches to keep the thorns from pressing in any deeper, but that's when it dawns on me that the mosquito man is standing over me. It reeks of rotten flesh and swamp water. The odor turns my stomach, and I feel my peanut butter crunch ice cream beg for release. I'm about to grant it its wish when I see something sharp dart toward me. I instinctively reach out to grab it, stopping its assault on my personal space.

"Wh . . . what is this?" I ask, still dizzied by the tackle into the thorn bushes. My eyes focus in and out before eventually settling on the rough, sandpaper-like object in my hands.

The proboscis.

Fight-or-flight takes over and my brain tries both options at the same time. I struggle to keep the proboscis from stabbing into me while simultaneously climbing out of the thorn bushes. The demon is too strong, however. I feel myself losing my grip. The proboscis is only inches away from impaling me. I'm as good as—

CRACK!

Neal brings a rotten tree limb down on the mosquito man's head, distracting it long enough for me to wriggle away from its proboscis. The hit shatters the limb but doesn't seem to do much damage to the demon. It turns to acknowledge Neal, but it doesn't attack him.

It cocks its head to the side and speaks, but its message doesn't come out of any mouth. Instead, the words are formed in the collective vibrations of the mosquito swarm that fills the air around us.

The words are strung together as the demon stares at Neal. "You are buzzzzt the witness. He will bezzzz one of many offerings yet to come."

I don't like the sound of that.

Content to put as much space between myself and the mosquito man, I crawl through the thorn bushes. I do even more harm to my skin and don't get very far for my troubles. The mosquito man reaches out with one of its appendages—really more of a barbed, stabby thing than a hand—and wraps it around my right ankle. The barbs slice through my socks and cut into me. I scream out, the pain almost unbearable.

I hear rustling behind me. I strain my neck to see what's coming next and a familiar face comes into view. It's Liam.

"No one tries to suck out my best friend's brain while I'm still standing!"

Liam launches himself at the mosquito man, delivering a dropkick to its midsection. The force is too much for the demon to take and it is thrown backward.

The demon rises in one unnaturally fluid motion and sets its eyes on Neal. The buzzing of the mosquitoes again becomes choreographed as words are formed within the vibrations.

"The witness has brouzzzzght forth multiple offerings. The feast shall sustain the hunger regardless of the emerging frost."

"Uh," Liam mumbles, looking all around. "What the heck was that?"

"The demon," I say, pulling myself up to my feet. "It speaks through the mosquitoes."

Neal's body shakes as he stands in the spotlight of the creature's vision. He looks for a path to escape, trying to will himself away, but he's grounded in the mud—forced to be the mosquito man's center of attention.

"Why does it keep looking at me?" he asks. "And why does it keep calling me 'the witness'?"

"I think I can answer that," Madelyn says, appearing behind me. She holds up her phone. "My artificial intelligence program has turned up some pretty interesting details."

The mosquito man howls. I don't think it cares very much for any details other than the one where our blood and brains are digesting in its belly.

14

If there are any additional howls brewing inside of the mosquito man, they are tamped down by Liam's fists. My best friend unleashes a flurry of punches on the demon. The tornado of strikes leaves the mosquito man little time to react, and it just has to absorb each and every blow. It stumbles backward. It tumbles forward. It grumbles as it sways from side to side. It just doesn't seem all that bothered by any of it.

Still, Liam keeps it occupied as Madelyn seizes the opportunity to tell Neal and me what she has learned.

"Apparently, this mosquito man creature has been seen in this area for centuries," she says, keeping one eye on the demon just in case it gets the best of Liam and we have to dodge its attacks. "But the really intriguing part is that there has always been exactly *one* person who has seen it during each of its waking periods and who is then allowed to live. The names of the witnesses have shown up in newspapers going back as far as 1717."

"The witness," Neal utters to himself. He's referring to what the mosquito man keeps calling him. "That's me. I'm the one who it said would live through this."

Madelyn continues. "And those names turned up an interesting connection." She pauses and then begins to list the names. "Zacharia Kemp. Anderson Kemp. Wally Kemp. George Kemp."

"They're all Kemps? But, that's my last name, too," Neal says, unhappy about the association.

Madelyn nods. "That's because all of those who have ever witnessed the mosquito man seem to be a part of your bloodline."

The news hits Neal like a sucker punch to the stomach. He sways.

"They were all your relatives," Madelyn continues. "You are connected to the creature on some supernatural level that I haven't quite figured out yet."

Neal stops swaying. "No. I don't want to be tied to that disgusting thing. Not anymore. This needs to stop. How do we kill it?"

Madelyn shakes her head. "I don't think we can. My program's final determination is that it is immortal—at least given what currently is known about it. It says that the demon's everywhere, which is what makes it impossible to kill."

I look up as Liam continues to pummel the mosquito man. I get the sneaking suspicion that Liam is faring so well in his fight with the demon because it is choosing not to fight back. In fact, it's not even defending itself. It's taking every punch Liam throws its way and seems no less powerful because of it.

I think back to the journal entries that Neal's grandfather wrote. There is definitely something we're missing. Something we're not seeing.

The demon was once whole and existed in an entirely different earthly form. The settlers who first discovered it managed to kill the demon and then burn its body. In doing so, the ashes that were created became what we now know as mosquitoes. The mosquitoes expanded across the globe—itsy-bitsy pieces of the demon spreading like a virus. The insects suck the blood of the living and then use the blood to fuel the demon's rebirth, giving it the strength to awaken and begin the cycle all over again.

So, if the mosquito man gets its power from the—

"Ow," I say, feeling the bite of a mosquito on my forearm. I slap at it, squashing it against my skin. At the same time, the demon lets out a small shriek and I look up to see it stagger. The mosquito man's staggering does not correspond with any action or reaction from Liam.

And that's when it dawns on me.

"You're attacking the wrong enemy!" I shout. "The mosquitoes! That's how we weaken it and force it into early hibernation! Squash the mosquitoes!"

Liam looks up and contemplates what I'm

telling him. He flattens out his clenched fists to use instead as flyswatters. He reaches up into the cloud of insects and claps, crushing a few dozen mosquitoes between his palms and fingers.

The demon cries out as if in pain. Its body convulses.

"Everyone," I continue, now further justified by the evidence, "kill as many mosquitoes as possible!"

The four of us ignore the demon and turn our attention to the horde of mosquitoes that fills the air.

We swat, slap, and strike as many of them as we can. Hundreds are killed. Each death we bring impacts the mosquito man physically. It reels, not even seeing the cat balancing along the tree branch above it.

Ricky and Denise leap down from the tree, landing in the middle of the action. They hold up one of their paws and slowly—and dramatically—extract their claws. Cats can't smile, but I would swear that this one is.

"There ain't a gig in the world that we're

better suited for than this bit of blast," Ricky says. "Let's rattle its cage, babe!"

Ricky and Denise leap into the air, swatting and swallowing as many mosquitoes as they can. With their feline dexterity and natural inclination to smack flying things out of the sky, the cat-trapped pair are like insect assassins, clearing the battlefield of hundreds of mosquitoes on their own.

The demon reels, screeching in pain and falling to the swampy ground in a distressed splash.

Finally, the mosquito man becomes an active participant in the fight. It springs up and knocks Ricky and Denise out of the air, forcing them headfirst into a nearby tree.

Thankfully they're spirits and can't be battered and bruised in the physical sense, but the demon doesn't stop there. It turns to Neal and me and lunges.

I react by reaching into my pocket and pulling out the squirt gun. The mosquito man takes a stream of holy water to the face and immediately stops its attack. It drops to the ground and presses its face into the swamp, trying desperately to wash away the water.

Liam steps up to the demon, laces his fingers together, and then cracks his knuckles. "The rest of you focus on the mosquitoes. I'll keep the big bug busy."

15

"Why am I a witness?" Neal asks as he claps, causing mosquitoes to splat between his hands. "How and why am I tied to this thing?"

Madelyn claps her hands together madly in the air. "I can only guess, but it would seem to make sense that your ancestor was the one who lit the pyre that burned the demon's original earthbound body. They were witness to its demise and therefore you are now tied by blood to forever witness its return."

I look down at the demon as Liam pins it to the muck with his strength. It's becoming weaker with each mosquito that we destroy. The only way to defeat it is to force it back into hibernation, but still, that will only be a temporary solution. Eventually it will return again, but at least if we can drive it away tonight, we can save any victims in the present day—including my dad—and have the necessary time to better research how we can vanquish it for good in the future.

"We are hurting it, but we have to think bigger," I say. "The first frost kills off the season's mosquitoes and that's what causes it to return to its hibernation. We need something that can really inflict some large-scale pain and keep it from killing anybody else this cycle."

While holding the demon to the ground, an idea seems to dawn on Liam. He reaches up to the mosquito man's head and grabs hold of its proboscis with both of his hands. He stands, rising to the balls of his feet, and yanks upward as hard as he can. At first, it looks like Liam is trying to pull a stubborn tree root out of the ground, but that all fades when the proboscis tears away from the demon's face. A lime green goo is left in its place, and the demon screams through the shared vibrations of the many mosquito wings surrounding us.

"The witness has bezzzztrayed the act of observation!" the quivering wings divulge.

With its back still on the ground, the

demon thrusts its appendages up into Liam's chest. Liam is hammered backward, tossed through the air with the speed of a high-powered drone. His spine hits the trunk of a full-grown black ash, snapping the hardwood tree in half. We all scatter to avoid the falling timber, which slams into the ground and rocks us like a miniature earthquake.

I run to check on Liam as he lays splayed out in the ankle-high swamp water. He gasps for breath.

"Are you okay?" I ask, grasping his left hand and squeezing. His right hand still holds onto the severed proboscis.

Liam grunts and groans as he sits up. "Never . . . better. Just need . . . a minute, is all."

Thankfully, it looks like he'll have more than a minute.

In fact, it looks like we'll have decades.

The mosquito man leaps to its feet and looks around in terror. It knows it has been defeated. Without speaking another word through its swarm or showing us a single sign of admission for the battle won, the demon sprints through the swamp and dives headfirst into a large pool of water. Although easily seven feet tall, it's swallowed up by the pool's murky depths. The cloud of mosquitoes begins to disperse, heading out into the night to feast and prepare for their maker's future return.

With Liam now back up on his feet, we all walk over to the edge of the pool and stare down into the water. We wait. Other than a few bubbles, there is no movement. The mosquito man is gone.

Liam sighs and tosses the severed proboscis into the center of the pool. It floats on the surface of the water. After a few moments, something stirs beneath it and then wormlike whiskers appear. The dark water becomes even darker as a large mouth opens and swallows the proboscis whole.

"Whoa!" Neal says, pointing down to the large brown bullhead catfish that swims happily around the perimeter of the pool, its appetite satisfied. "I bet that's my grandfather's hornpout! The one he was coming out here to catch all those years ago!"

I smile and nudge Liam with my elbow. "See. I told you—involving Neal would really put a nice bow on this whole package."

Liam rolls his eyes and steps away from the pool. "As long as he doesn't tell anyone else about what I am and what we do, we're more than good."

Neal extends his hand to Liam. "Your secret is safe with me. But if that thing ever comes back in my lifetime, you best believe I'm calling each and every one of you."

"Don't worry, we'll be there," I say, digging into my pocket and retrieving my phone. "And the next time it shows up, we'll be better prepared to kill it once and for all."

I open up my phone settings and reactivate my tracking app. My dad is probably worried sick. And when he gets a good look at me—how scraped up I am from the thorns and from battling the mosquito man—he's going to realize that his concerns were justified. I guess I had better get ready to tell him the truth about what I do in my spare time. I'm sure I can find some fun things to do in the solitary confinement of my bedroom for the next ten years.

We head back the way we came through the swamp until we reach dry land. We emerge from the foliage onto the side of the road across from Lickity Splits. My dad's cruiser is parked there. He is sitting in the driver's seat, impatiently tapping his fingers against the steering wheel. Ricky and Denise say their goodbyes and disappear into the underbrush, slinking through the night and hoping to remain unseen by my father's probing eyes.

My dad leaps out of his cruiser and runs around to meet us as we push through the thorn bushes. He looks me up and down. His eyes narrow and I can see him inhale a lungful of air. He's readying himself to yell at me.

Much to my surprise, Neal steps up. He puts himself between my dad and me. "Sir, I know you're angry at Damon, but before you show him any of that anger, can I explain what he's been doing?"

I nervously watch as my dad considers what he is being asked. He doesn't know Neal, so if it were Liam or Madelyn who interrupted my impending scolding, I think his response would be much different.

"Okay," he says, his jaw clenching as he swallows down his looming lecture. "I'm listening."

"My name is Neal Kemp, sir. I'm in the Chickadee Scouts with Damon. I did a really dense thing earlier today, and it was your son and his friends who helped me in a big way."

I don't know where Neal is going with this not-exactly-truthful explanation, but my dad's stiff posture is already softening.

"I decided to go for a hike on my own in the swamps," he continues, his story pouring out of him like ice cream from the Lickity Splits soft-serve machines. "I didn't bring any of my gear—not even a compass, which is not what the Chickadees taught me at all—and I got lost when it started to get dark. I had seen Damon and his friends at the ice cream stand, so I knew they were nearby. I panicked and called him to tell him I was in trouble, and they hiked out to my location and helped me back. I was so scared that I'd be stuck out here all night and that my parents would ground me for the rest of the summer. I am so embarrassed, and I'm sorry that I pulled him into all of this. I didn't mean to get anybody into trouble."

My dad studies Neal with his eyes and then turns to me. "Is this true, Damon?"

I hesitate to respond. Liam pokes me in the back, jump-starting an answer. "Yeah. I shut off my tracking app because I knew how mad you'd be at me for going out in the swamps. I was hoping we could find Neal quickly and then make it out before you noticed, but . . . it took us longer than I thought it would. I accept whatever punishment is coming my way."

My dad is silent as he considers everything he has been told. It seems like a week passes us by before he eventually responds. I hate having to lie to him, but what we're doing—hunting demons—it helps people. If and when my dad finds out, my demon hunting days are so over.

My dad nods. "We'll talk about that later," he says, pointing back at his cruiser. "Everyone get in. I'll take you all home. Your parents are probably just as worried as I was."

We silently climb into the cruiser—me in the front seat and everyone else in the back—and buckle ourselves into place. My dad shifts the car into drive and prepares to merge onto the road, but then he stops himself and turns back to us.

"Whose cat was that?" he asks.

ABOUT THE AUTHOR

When not writing in his spiral notebooks, Jason M. Burns can be found outside getting his tattoo-covered arms dirty where he spends the warmer months hybridizing daylilies and tending to his koi pond. Type A even when typing, he has written and created a number of critically-acclaimed and commercially successful comic book series and graphic novels, including *Magical Pet Vet* and *Jericho: Season 3*, which appeared on the *New York Times* Best Sellers list. He has spearheaded book lines for *Sesame Street* and the DreamWorks Animation stable of titles and most recently served as Chief Creative Officer for Neymar Jr. Comics, the publishing company of international soccer star Neymar Jr. There his writing was translated across six languages and reached over forty million people worldwide. In addition to comic books, Burns also works in Hollywood where he has a number of television and film projects in development. He is also co-host of the popular podcast series *What About*, which he produces alongside actor Danny Nucci (*Titanic*, *The Fosters*).

Burns lives in Massachusetts with his wife, two children, and a trio of rescue dogs with unnecessarily silly names, Bark W. Grizwold, Maisy Gray, and Bad Bad Leroy Brown.